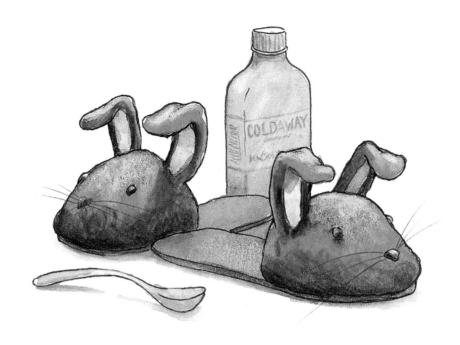

Miss Malarkey Won't Be in Today

Miss Malarkey Won't Be in Today

Judy Finchler
Illustrations by Kevin O'Malley

Walker and Company ✺ New York

First published in the United States of America in 1998 by Walker Publishing Company, Inc.

Published simultaneously in Canada by Thomas Allen & Son Canada, Limited, Markham, Ontario

Library of Congress Cataloging-in-Publication Data
Finchler, Judy.
Miss Malarkey won't be in today/Judy Finchler; illustrations by Kevin O'Malley.
p.   cm.
Summary: A teacher imagines the chaos that takes place when she stays home one day because she is sick.
ISBN 0-8027-8652-9 (hardcover) −0-8027-8653-7 (reinforced)
[1. Teachers–Fiction. 2. Sick–Fiction. 3. Schools–Fiction.]
I. O'Malley, Kevin, 1961– ill. II. Title.
PZ7.F495666M1 1998
[E]—dc21
                                              97-48729
                                                CIP
                                                 AC

Book design by Sophie Ye Chin

Printed in Hong Kong
10 9 8 7 6 5 4 3 2

To all my children
Todd and Susan, Lauren and Jim,
and the children of
Paterson School 15. —J. F.

To all my children's teachers . . .
give them all A's! —K. O.

I couldn't go to school this morning,
not with a fever of **103.2.**

I had to call Principal Wiggins.

Principal Wiggins doesn't *like* it
when a teacher calls in sick.

Then he has to find a substitute.

He hates finding substitutes.

Oh,

and the last substitute he found

for Mrs. Boba's class didn't exactly work out.

My poor class!

What if he called Mr. Doberman?

That guy is so tough he even scares me.

Or he might have called Mrs. Ungerware.

The kids call her Mrs. *Underwear*.

Once my kids start laughing, they'll never stop.

Mrs. *Underwear* won't be able

to get anything done.

Oh, I hope he didn't call Mr. Lemonjello.

Mr. Lemonjello

is

such a

n e r v o u s

man.

Sometimes my kids

can be a handful.

He'll be scared **stiff** if they let the iguana out of its cage.

He'll never be able to handle them in music class. They'll crank up the **volume.**

They'll dance on the desks.
They'll swing from the lights.

And then they'll all ask to go to the bathroom at the same time.

At the same time!

I have to get to school.

Right now!

Everyone looks okay.

Better than I imagined.

Better behaved than they are for me?

Oh, my class!

Oh, the bell!

Oh, my head!

"Miss Malarkey, where were you today?"
"Did Mr. Wiggins make you sit out here?"

"Oh, no. I didn't feel very well today,
        but I've been worried sick about everybody."

"We're fine, but you look terrible."
"Feel her head. Maybe she needs an ice pack."
"Let's take her to the nurse in case
        she needs to throw up."

"*Don't worry,* Miss Malarkey.
You just stay home and rest up."

"And if Mrs. Berpur is
our teacher tomorrow,
we'll take care of everything."

Oh no, not Ima Berpur!